MW01087536

Bunny and Clyde

Megan McDonald

illustrated by Scott Nash

CANDLEWICK PRESS

For Blanche Woolls—
teacher, mentor, friend
MM

To Norah, Poppa John, and Gigi
SN

First edition 2024

Library of Congress Catalog Card Number 2023943707
ISBN 978-1-5362-2873-1

24 25 26 27 28 29 FRS 10 9 8 7 6 5 4 3 2 1

Printed in Altona, Manitoba, Canada

This book was typeset in Plantin MT Pro.
The illustrations were created digitally.

Candlewick Press
99 Dover Street
Somerville, Massachusetts 02144

www.candlewick.com

Contents

-1-
No Good

Bunny and Clyde were tired of being good.

Every day Maw-Maw kissed Bunny and said, “Be good.” So Bunny was.

Every day Paw-Paw hugged Clyde and said, “Mind your manners.” So Clyde did.

Every day at school, their teacher told them, "Raise your hands! Follow directions! Use inside voices!" So they did.

But Bunny and Clyde were tired of making their beds. They were tired of saying please and thank you. They were tired of keeping burps to themselves.

They were done playing nice. They were done being told what to do.

One morning on their way down the sidewalk, Bunny spotted a bubble gum comic. She picked it up. Clyde spotted an old bottle cap. He picked it up. Along came Old Lady Murphy. She patted each of them on the head and said, “What a pair of good little bunnies!”

Bunny hated being patted on the head. Clyde hated being called a good little bunny. He was a chipmunk!

"She thinks we're picking up trash," said Clyde.

"She doesn't even know we're treasure hunting," said Bunny.

And so on that one perfect Minnesota morning, Bunny said to Clyde, "Let's be bad for once!"

"Bad to the bone," said Clyde.

There was only one problem. Up

to now, Bunny and Clyde had always been good. The two goodniks did not have the first clue how to be bad.

But they did know one thing. When a baffled bunny was looking to learn something, when a curious chipmunk needed information, there was only one place to go.

"Are you thinking what I'm thinking?" asked Bunny.

"Are you thinking what I'm thinking?" asked Clyde.

"To the library!" said Bunny and Clyde at the same time.

FINEST FOODS
FRESH FRUIT & VEGETABLES
BANANAS
PEARS
-6¢-
I ♥ READING

-2-
Bad Books

Bunny and Clyde grabbed their library cards and the I ♥ READING tote. They hopped on their shiny red tandem bike and pedaled to the library. Racing up the steps and through the big glass door, they found their friend Rowena working at the front desk.

"Rowena!" said Bunny, sidling up to the counter. "Do you have any, um, bad books?"

Rowena was loading books onto a cart. "As a famous writer once said, 'Life is too short for bad books.' I like to think that the library is full of *good* books."

"Just point us to the bad section," said Bunny. She almost added *please* but caught herself just in time.

"Yeah, there must be books with bad stuff somewhere in this joint," said Clyde.

Rowena looked stumped. And someone who works in a library is almost never stumped.

She hemmed and hawed and hawed and hemmed and scratched her head with her wing. "Aha!" she said at last. "Follow me."

Rowena led them through the stacks to a row marked 500. "Try the 551s."

As soon as Rowena left, Bunny and Clyde pawed through the books on the shelves. Volcanoes! Earthquakes! Hurricanes! Tornadoes!

"Bad, bad, bad, and bad," said Bunny.

"But not the kind of bad we're looking for," said Clyde.

They were about to give up when Clyde noticed mountains of picture books scattered all over the floor of

the library's Young Readers room.

"What a mess!" said Clyde.

"These books should be lined up on the shelves," said Bunny. "Spine out!"

"Maybe there are bad books somewhere in this mess," said Clyde.

Bunny hunted through heaps and heaps of books. Clyde pored over piles and piles of books. "All these books have *good* and *love* and *hugs* in the titles."

"All these books have pink unicorns and sparkly rainbows," said Bunny.

Bunny and Clyde dug to the bottom of the biggest pile. At last!

They took their haul up to the front counter. "Wow!" said Rowena. "You two are my best readers. Let's see what we have here."

HAMSTE
GANGSTERS
HIJINKS
UNFLOWER
SEEDS
UNFLOWER
SEEDS

Rowena clucked as she checked out their books. "Hmm. Interesting choices. Some bunny's up to some hijinks," she said with a twinkle.

Bunny flushed pink all the way to the tips of her ears. A shifty-eyed Clyde shuffled his feet.

Bunny hurried to hide the loot in the I ♥ READING tote. Clyde plunked down five pennies for a bookmark.

Rowena picked up a penny and studied the back of it. “Hey! This is a whole-wheat penny. These are rare, like a hundred years old. I bet it’s worth a pretty penny!”

Bunny and Clyde were only half-listening.

"This is going in my piggy bank at home. You're welcome to come see it anytime. It's almost full, but I'm sure I can squeeze in one more." She pulled a penny from her pocket to replace it.

"Happy reading!" she called, but Bunny and Clyde were already out the door, on their way to being bad.

-3-

A Fine Mess

At Bunny's house, Bunny and Clyde spread their library loot all over the floor, ready to bone up on being bad. Bunny read *Interrupting Chicken*. Clyde read *The Tale of Two Bad Mice*.

Bunny held up the chicken book. "This squawking chicken won't stop interrupting!"

"You think *that's* bad," said Clyde. "These two mice went on a crime spree."

Bunny picked up a book with a bulgy-eyed black cat. "Let's try this one."

Clyde flattened his ears. Clyde fluffed his tail. Clyde made a *chuck-chuck* sound. "You know how I feel about cats!" said Clyde.

"C'mon. Don't be a scaredy-cat.

RHINO
BADGER

It's just a cartoon cat in a book."

"Stop saying *c-a-t*," said Clyde with a shiver.

"You know I'm just *kitten* around," said Bunny.

Clyde rolled his eyes. "Fine. Just read the book."

Together they read *Bad Kitty*.

"That cat is one big temper tantrum," said Bunny. "And she eats up homework and claws the curtains."

"That *is* bad," said Clyde. "Oops. I mean good."

In no time, Bunny and Clyde were ready to be bad. They would be two bad apples, rotten to the core.

"What should we do first?" asked Clyde.

Bunny twisted her whiskers. "Mess up my room!" she said.

Bunny and Clyde flew upstairs. Bunny's room was neat as a pin.

Bunny took books off the shelf and put them back in *un*-alphabetical order. Clyde tore a poster off the wall. Bunny knocked over her basket of

stuffed animals. Clyde tossed a pair of socks on the floor.

“This is a fine mess,” Bunny said with awe.

“Roger that,” said Clyde.

“Are we bad yet?” asked Bunny.

"Let's be badder," said Clyde.

Bunny dumped out a box of sixty-four crayons. "Let's color on the walls!"

Bunny drew a sunflower. Clyde drew a rainbow.

"That's a sunny sunflower," said Clyde, admiring Bunny's art.

"That's a rosy rainbow," said Bunny, admiring Clyde's art.

"Ack! This is *not* bad," said Clyde. He drew a four-eyed monster cat with a Gremlin Green crayon. Bunny drew a fang-toothed vampire bunny in Atomic Purple.

"Are we bad yet?" asked Bunny.

"Let's be badder," said Clyde.

They ran down to the kitchen. Clyde drank milk right out of the carton. Bunny tore her chore chart in half. Clyde spilled marbles from the Swear Jar. Bunny did not even compost her mushy apple core.

Last but not least, they raided the secret stash of penny candy that Maw-Maw had hidden under the kitchen sink. Bunny stuffed her pockets with sour balls and saltwater taffy, root-beer barrels and butterscotch

buttons. Clyde stuffed his cheeks with love hearts and lemon drops, rainbow wheels and raspberry rounds.

"Another fine mess," said Bunny.

"We're really getting the hang of this being bad stuff," said Clyde.

Just then, they heard a key jangle in the front door. The door squeaked open. Nails clicked across the floor.

"Maw-Maw!" whispered Bunny, her eyes wide.

"Let's scram," whispered Clyde. They hightailed it out the back door, making off with the penny candy.

Bunny and Clyde leaned against the old shed out back. Clyde caught his breath.

"Are you thinking what I'm thinking?" asked Bunny.

"Are you thinking what I'm

thinking?" asked Clyde.

"Secret hideout!" they said at the same time.

Just then, Maw-Maw called them inside. *Uh-oh.*

Bunny and Clyde picked up marbles and scrubbed off crayon till their paws ached.

SUNFLOWER SEEDS
SUNFLOWER SEEDS

-4-

Experience

The very next day, Bunny and Clyde were feeling quite crafty. They turned Bunny's old shed into a super-secret hideout. Bunny hung carrot curtains in the window. Clyde strung twinkly lights from the rafters. Bunny stacked the not-yet-overdue library books.

Clyde dumped the secret stash of penny candy into a bucket. They tacked up a sign on the door that said GROWN-UPS KEEP OUT!

Bunny chewed on a licorice whip. Clyde blew on a red-hot fireball. "All bad guys have a secret hideout," said Clyde.

"Now we can plan something big," said a satisfied Bunny, propping her big bunny feet up on a bag of birdseed.

"Now we can plan something bad," said Clyde. He shifted the fireball from cheek to cheek. "We've got a secret hideout. We've got book smarts. But something's missing."

"A beanbag chair?"

"No," said Clyde.

"More penny candy?" asked Bunny, biting into her candy necklace. "Because we're already out of rock candy."

"No," said Clyde. *"Experience."*

"Experience? What's experience?" asked Bunny, stopping mid-chew.

"It means to get good at something. Like getting good at being bad."

"How about if we practice being bad on our friends?" Bunny suggested.

"Perfect," said Clyde. "No one will ever think it's us."

"Experience, here we come," said Bunny.

"Let's blow this popcorn stand," said Clyde.

★ ★ ★

Bunny and Clyde crawled out of their hideout and squinted in the bright sunshine. Clyde did his usual cat scan to make sure no sneaky cats were lurking about.

"Look!" Bunny pointed. "*Catty*-corner across the street."

Clyde frowned, trying to ignore the bad word. Across the street, sunny yellow flowers peppered Darby's yard under the squirrel's favorite oak tree.

"Darby's flowers look as happy as daisies," said Bunny.

"Darby's flowers always cheer me right up," said Clyde.

Just then, Bunny and Clyde caught themselves enjoying the flowers. Clyde narrowed his eyes. "Show-offs," he spat, trying to sound bad.

"Are you thinking what I'm thinking?" asked Bunny.

"Are you thinking what I'm thinking?" asked Clyde.

Bunny and Clyde raced across to Darby's yard. They started yanking up yellow flowers.

“Flowers are for goody-goodies,” said Bunny.

“These oopsy-daisies are going down,” said Clyde.

They plucked golden petals. They ripped out lion-toothed leaves. They dug up roots until they were covered from head to toe in dirt.

"We're baaad!" said Bunny.

"Bad to the bone," said Clyde.

"Two bad apples," said Bunny.

"Rotten to the core," said Clyde.

Bunny and Clyde were so busy being bad that their ears did not perk up at the sound of a squirrel coming up behind them.

"Aha!" cried Darby. Her eyes grew wide when she saw what they had done. She let out a *kuk-kuk* sound. "Bunny and Clyde! What on earth did you two do?"

Bunny's cottontail itched and twitched. Clyde's fur stood on end. "It wasn't us!" they said at the same time.

But it was no use. Bunny and Clyde were caught red-handed. There was no way to weasel out of this one.

"Now don't pretend it wasn't you," said Darby.

Bunny's heart fluttered. "It was us," she couldn't help admitting.

"We dug up all your yellow flowers," said Clyde.

Bunny hung her head. Clyde's tail drooped.

"Aren't you two the sweetest?" Darby cooed.

"Did she say sweetest?" said Bunny.

"I think she means baddest," said Clyde.

"I know a good deed when I see one," Darby went on. "No more dandelions. Don't you just hate those pesky weeds? They take over my whole yard!"

Dandelions? Pesky? Weeds?

"Um, sure," said Bunny, ignoring her racing heart. "Everybody knows dandelions are weeds. Right, Clyde?"

"Of course!" Clyde agreed. "We, um, thought we'd weed your yard for you."

"Thank you for all your hard work," said Darby.

"Um, you're welcome?" said Clyde.

Bunny and Clyde slumped back down the street toward their hideout.

"We *thought* we were bad," said Bunny. "How did we end up doing a good deed?"

"Beats me," said Clyde.

"Let's face it," said Bunny. "We are not very good at being bad."

"We stink," said Clyde, pinching his nose to make the P.U. sign.

"That sure was a heart-racing experience," said Bunny. Her heart was still pounding.

On their way back to the hideout, they passed Thornton's rosebushes. The perfect prize-winning roses seemed to scoff at them.

"Hey!" said Bunny. "Those flowers are roses. *Roses* aren't weeds."

"Even *we* know that," said Clyde.

“Are you thinking what I’m thinking?” asked Bunny.

“Are you thinking what I’m thinking?” asked Clyde.

“Tonight!” said Bunny.

“Tonight!” said Clyde.

-5-

First Frost

That night, Bunny and Clyde (yes, even Clyde) dressed like cat burglars to blend into the dark. They stuffed their backpacks with supplies for making mischief. They silently stole down the street to Thornton's house.

Bunny looked left. Clyde looked right. Not a possum in sight. Not even a c-a-t.

"This time we don't get caught," said Clyde.

Bunny and Clyde pulled something out of their backpacks. Toilet paper! Rolls and rolls of toilet paper. They hopped over the fence. TP time! They tossed toilet paper rolls in the air. They wound toilet paper around and around the roses.

Swoosh. “What was that?” Bunny ducked behind a rosebush. It was just the wind stirring up a pile of leaves.

Whoosh. “What was that?” Clyde darted behind a tree trunk. It was just Orson, the old hoot owl, rustling the pine needles as he landed in the tall tree.

Bunny and Clyde shivered.

"My tummy feels funny," Bunny whispered.

"It's just a case of the willies," Clyde whispered back.

All of a sudden, a light went on in Thornton's house. Bunny and Clyde froze. The hair on the back of their necks stood up. Through the window, they could see Thornton shuffling about the kitchen. Luckily Thornton didn't notice the sneaky rabbit or the clever chipmunk crouched in the dark behind a ghostly rosebush.

The light clicked off. Bunny and Clyde breathed a sigh of relief.

They continued TP-ing each rosebush until every last rose in the

garden was mummified. The night turned cold. *Minnesota* cold.

"I'm chilled to the bone," said Bunny. "Let's get outta here."

"My whiskers are freezing," said Clyde. "Let's scram."

They made tracks down the street. A trail of toilet paper stuck to Clyde's tail. It followed him all the way back to the hideout.

"Let's bunk here tonight," said Clyde.

Bunny curled up under a quilt. "We are bad," she said, teeth chattering.

Clyde bundled under a blanket. "So bad," he said, popping a fuzzy, half-melted fireball from his pocket into his mouth.

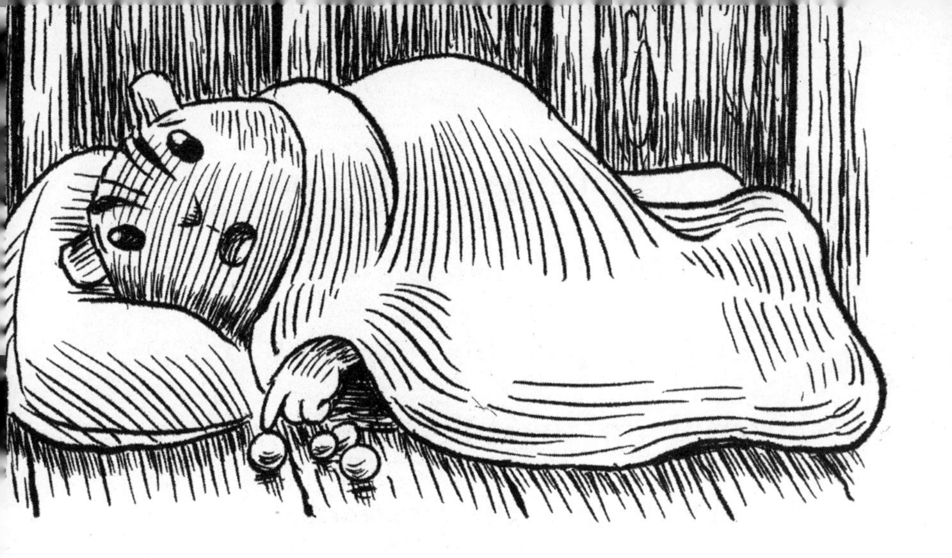

"That sure was a hair-raising experience," said Bunny.

Clyde nodded in agreement. Bunny chewed on her candy necklace.

That night, Bunny could hardly sleep a wink. Clyde was up half the night, watching fingers of frost make icy pictures on the windows.

★ ★ ★

The next morning, Bunny and Clyde couldn't wait to spy on Thornton and see that possum's reaction. They skittered up the hill and down the slippery slope of the sidewalk.

Thornton was already on the sidewalk, hands on hips. He spied them from halfway down the block.

There was nowhere to run, nowhere to hide.

"Bunny Elizabeth Parker and Clyde Chestnut Wheelbarrow!" hissed Thornton. "I was just on my way to speak with you."

Gulp. Bunny felt like she had swallowed a sour ball.

"Word on the street is that you two are responsible for this." Thornton *tsk*ed and pointed to his toilet-papered rosebushes.

Orson. That old hoot owl sure is a tattletale.

Bunny's tummy flippity-flopped. Clyde's heart hopscotched.

Bunny tried to change the subject. "Sure was cold last night, huh?" she said. They could see her breath in the air.

"First frost!" Clyde chimed in, rubbing his paws together.

"How did you know it was going to frost?" asked Thornton.

"I could feel it in my whiskers," said Clyde.

"I had no idea we were in for a

frost," said Thornton. He looked a bit shaken. "If you two hadn't covered my roses like a blanket, I could have lost every last rosebud in my garden."

Bunny looked at Clyde. Clyde looked at Bunny.

Frost? Cover? Blanket?

"How can I ever thank you?" asked Thornton.

"Um, you're welcome?" said Clyde.

They waved goodbye as fast as they could.

"Strike two," said Clyde.

"My tummy feels wibbly-wobbly," said Bunny. "And my hind legs are all herky-jerky."

"It's just a case of the colly-wobbles," said Clyde.

"I thought being bad would make me feel better," said Bunny.

"I guess we're not good at being bad yet," Clyde concluded.

-6-
Brush with Badness

On the way back to their hideout, Bunny and Clyde passed their friend Hamilton riding his new bike in his driveway. It had a big basket in front, silver streamers on the handlebars, and a shiny bike horn. His training

wheels wobbled and his bushy tail shook back and forth as he rode in circles.

"Looking good!" called Bunny.

"Happy four-wheeling, Hamilton!" said Clyde.

Toot-toot! Hamilton honked his horn happily in reply.

"Hamilton sure loves that new bike," said Bunny.

"That empty basket is just crying out for something," said Clyde.

"Are you thinking what I'm thinking?" asked Bunny.

"Are you thinking what I'm thinking?" asked Clyde.

"Let's be bad once and for all," said Bunny, pointing to her backpack.

Bunny and Clyde hid behind a clump of chokecherry. They watched and waited until Hamilton went inside.

Bunny and Clyde crept over to Hamilton's bike. Clyde dug to the bottom of Bunny's backpack. They sneakily placed something in the basket.

"Run!" cried Bunny. They ran back to the chokecherry and crouched behind it. Bunny gave Clyde an underhanded high five.

"Hamilton is going to get a big surprise," said Bunny, giggling. "A surprise with eight eyes!"

"We'll scare the stink right out of that skunk," said Clyde.

"Bad at last!" said Bunny.

"Bad to the bone," said Clyde.

Just then, Hamilton skipped down the driveway. Hamilton picked up his bike. Hamilton peered at the thing in his bike basket.

"Here it comes. The scream," whispered Bunny.

But Hamilton did not scream. He jumped back in surprise. All the hairs on his back stood up straight. He raised his tail and . . .

"Back away!" said Clyde. "He's going to spray!"

"Hamilton! Wait!" cried Bunny, coming out of hiding with Clyde.

Hamilton peered at the thing up close. He let his tail down. "Bunny and Clyde? I should have known it was you."

Bunny looked at Clyde. Clyde looked at Bunny.

Hamilton started laughing. "For a second there, you two almost had me fooled! I can't believe you found a fake wolf spider for me. How did you know I could use this for my science project, *Diary of a Spider*?"

"Your what?" asked Bunny. Clyde nudged her with his elbow. "Oh! Right! Our science unit . . ."

"On nocturnal animals—owls, bats, and spiders," Clyde continued.

"Thanks, guys," said Hamilton. "Extra credit, here I come."

"Great," said Bunny.

"Just great," said Clyde.

Bunny and Clyde were down in the dumps. They were in a slump.

"Just when we thought we were bad," said Clyde.

"Why does everything bad we do

turn out to be good?" Bunny moaned.

"For a minute there, we did have a brush with badness," Clyde pointed out.

"At least we got some good experience," said Bunny.

"You mean *bad* experience," said Clyde.

"Let's go experience some penny candy at the hideout," said Bunny.

"You read my mind," said Clyde.

-7-

Wanted: Dead or Alive

Back at the hideout, Bunny and Clyde were thick as thieves. Bunny popped a sour ball in her mouth. Clyde ate three candy buttons in a row.

At last, Bunny and Clyde had something that was sorely missing.

They had Experience.

"Know something?" said Bunny with a satisfied burp. "Being bad is the *cat's* pajamas."

"Don't start with me!" said Clyde. They both laughed their heads off.

"Nobody even knows we were bad," said Clyde.

"Is being bad any good if nobody knows about it?" asked Bunny.

"Nope," said Clyde. "We need a bad rap all over town."

"We'll be like those bad guys on posters at the post office," said Bunny. "*Wanted.*"

"That's it!" said Clyde. "We should make our own Wanted poster."

Bunny got out construction paper. Clyde got out crayons and markers.

Bunny gave herself an eye patch and a tattoo. Clyde gave himself a scar with permanent marker. A marker they borrowed *without asking*.

They tacked the poster up outside their hideout.

"Hmm," said Clyde. "Are you seeing what I'm seeing?"

"Tricks, pranks, and a flower fiasco. Not much of a résumé," said Bunny. "We need something bigger."

"Something badder," said Clyde.

What was the biggest, baddest thing they could think of?

"I need more brain food," said Bunny, heading back into the hideout. "Pass the peppermints."

Clyde turned the empty bag upside down. "We're all out of penny candy," he said, pointing to the last peppermint lumps stuffed in his chubby cheeks. "And I spent my last pennies on that bookmark at the library."

"It did say EVERYBUNNY LOVES READING," said Bunny.

Clyde smiled a crooked smile.

"I know that look!" said Bunny. "That's your I've-got-an-idea look. Your ten-most-wanted look."

"Think about it," said Clyde. "To get penny candy, we need pennies. And to get pennies, we need . . ."

Bunny twirled her whiskers until they looked like licorice twists.

Now that Bunny and Clyde had Experience, they could think big. They could think bad. In no time, they came up with the biggest, baddest thing they could imagine.

DING!

"Are you thinking what I'm thinking?" asked Bunny.

"Are you thinking what I'm thinking?" asked Clyde.

"A bank job!" cried Bunny and Clyde at the same time.

"Let's rob a bank!" said Bunny.

"Now you're talking," said Clyde.

So Bunny and Clyde set out to rob a bank.

★ ★ ★

Clyde made a list of stuff they would need to rob a bank.

Bunny looked at the list. “Number one. Getaway car.” She stopped to think. “Before we find a getaway car, we’ll need to learn how to drive.”

“Drat. I didn’t think of that,” said Clyde.

“How about we use our tandem bike for the getaway car?” asked Bunny.

"Good idea, Bunny," said Clyde.

"Number two," said Bunny. "Disguises. Do you have a mask? Fake beard? Sunglasses?"

Clyde did not. So Bunny and Clyde made paper-plate masks.

"I'll be a chipmunk," said Bunny.

"And I'll be a bunny," said Clyde. "Nobody will ever know it's us."

"Don't we need a name for our duo?" asked Bunny. "Like the . . . Minnesota Twins? Or the Midwest Mole Rats?"

"Let's stick with Bunny and

Clyde," said Clyde. "What's next on the list?"

"Number three. A knife," said Bunny. "Eep!" She squeaked in alarm. "We don't want to hurt anyone! We just want to pick up a little scratch. You know, penny-candy money."

"Relax," said Clyde. "It's just to pick a lock."

"In that case, how about a spatula? Frying pan? Rolling pin?"

"Maybe just a spoon," said Clyde.

Bunny added a spoon to her backpack.

Bunny went down the list. "Number four. Dewlap bag. What's a dewlap bag?"

"No idea," said Clyde. "But all good bank robbers in the olden days, like Bonnie and Clyde, had them. Maybe it's for holding all the loot."

"You mean all *bad* bank robbers had them," said Bunny.

Bunny searched around the hideout. "How about we use the *I Love Reading* tote bag? For the loot."

"Roger that," said Clyde. "Nobody will know that it's loot. They'll just think we're returning our library books." Bunny snort-laughed at that one.

"Ready to rob a bank?" asked Clyde.

"One more teeny-tiny detail," said Bunny. "What bank should we rob?"

"I know just the one," said Clyde.

-8-

Mask Up!

The next day, Bunny snuck up behind Clyde. “Hand over all your loot,” she hissed.

“Eesh!” Clyde yelped. He almost jumped out of his fur.

"Don't worry. It's just me, Bunny," said Bunny. "I wouldn't really take your money, even if you had any."

"Phew," said Clyde, his heart still racing. "I thought you were a c-a-t."

Bunny and Clyde hopped on their getaway bike. Bunny checked and double-checked her backpack to make sure she had the spoon. Clyde slung the I ♥ READING tote over his shoulder. They put on their paper-plate masks. They tore down the street full speed ahead.

First Darby waved. "Hi, Bunny! Hi, Clyde!"

Then Thornton called out, "Hello there, Bunny. Clyde."

Then Hamilton hallooed at them. "Hey, friends. Bunny and Clyde!"

"How do they know it's us?" asked Bunny.

"Don't worry. They think you're Clyde and I'm Bunny," said Clyde.

They looked up and down the street. The coast was clear. The clouds in the sky were lowering. A thrill of danger crackled in the air.

"Are you sure this is the way to the bank?" asked Bunny.

"Trust me," said Clyde.

Clyde huffed and puffed and pedaled until Bunny signaled him to stop. He slammed on the brakes.

They pushed their masks up on their heads. Bunny gazed at the building before them. It looked taller than usual. The windows and front door seemed to make a foreboding face at her.

"Hey. This isn't a bank," said Bunny. "This is Rowena's house."

"Are you thinking what I'm thinking?" asked Clyde.

"I don't think I am," said a confused Bunny.

"Piggy bank," Clyde whispered.

"Oh! Good thinking," said Bunny.

“I forgot Rowena said she had a stash of cash in that piggy bank of hers.”

“Do you think she’s home?” asked Clyde.

"Her bike is still there," said Bunny. "That could mean she hasn't left for the library yet."

Old Man Raccoon tapped his cane on the sidewalk. A dog crossed the street. Somebody whizzed past them on a skateboard.

"We better lay low for a while," said Clyde. "There are eyes everywhere."

"Stakeout time," said Bunny. She pulled in behind a shady-looking bush with red berries. "We can watch the house from here until the heat dies down."

Bunny and Clyde waited. And waited. No Rowena. They waited some more. No Rowena. Clyde started to think about the bank job. "What will you buy with all your loot?"

"Jawbreakers and jelly beans and jolly pops," said Bunny. "You?"

"The sky's the limit," said Clyde.

Bunny and Clyde heard a door slam. Then the squeak of bike tires.

"There goes Rowena!" said Bunny.

"She's off to the library," said Clyde.

At last it was time.

“Mask up!” said Clyde. Bunny put on her chipmunk mask. Clyde put on his bunny mask. They stashed the getaway bike behind the winterberry bush.

“Ready or not . . .” said Bunny.

“Here we come!” said Clyde.

-9-

The Bank Job

Bunny and Clyde had been to Rowena's house more times than you could count on one paw. But this time felt different.

Even though the sun was out, Bunny had cold feet. She felt a chill from the tips of her ears to her cottontail. "Are you sure about this?" Bunny asked Clyde.

"We cased the joint first, didn't we?" said Clyde. "Like all good bank robbers do."

Bunny and Clyde slunk across the yard. They snuck around to the back door. *Eureka!* It was unlocked. Silently, they opened it and slipped inside.

Some might call this breaking and

entering. But all they were doing was entering. Bunny and Clyde didn't break a thing. *Yet.*

"We're a shoo-in," said Bunny, trying not to sound nervous.

"This bird's not gonna know what hit her," said Clyde, trying to sound confident.

Just then, Bunny heard a creaky-floor sound. She ducked under a table.

Just then, Clyde heard a squeaky-door sound. He dashed behind a curtain.

Bunny's ears were on high alert. Clyde's ears flattened and his tail bristled.

"False alarm," said Clyde, letting go a big breath.

Bunny came out from under the table. She knocked into a vase. It wibble-wobbled. *Whoa!* It tipple-toppled until—*whoosh!* Clyde caught it just in time.

“Phew,” said Bunny. “That was a close one.”

They had almost committed entering and breaking.

Bunny and Clyde tiptoed across the carpet.

They sneaked up the stairs.

They stole down the hall to Rowena's room. Bunny and Clyde took one last furtive glance behind them, then skittered inside.

There it was.

At last.

The bank.

The piggy bank, in its place of honor on the dresser top.

Pink and plump and perfect, it gleamed like a prize trophy.

"Time for some safecracking!" said Clyde.

Bunny pulled the spoon from her backpack and handed it to Clyde. She stuck her head out the door to keep watch.

Clyde slid the flat end of the spoon into the coin slot at just the right angle. He tilted the piggy bank upside down. Out slid a penny. Then two more pennies. Then three. Then a bus token and a stray nickel.

"Shoo-be-doo-be-doo-wah!" cried Bunny.

In no time, it was raining money. Coppery coins piled up on the bed. Bunny spied the old whole-wheat penny. And a very special silver dollar gleamed at the top of the pile.

"Look at all this lettuce in the fridge!" said Clyde. "Hand me the dewlap bag. Let's load up this loot, then cheese it on outta here."

"Shh!" Bunny warned. "I hear something."

Clyde heard it too.

Now, it's true that houses do make a lot of noises. But this was not a house creak or squeak. This was not a house moan or groan.

"Footsteps!" whispered Bunny.

"Ro-we-na!" sputtered Clyde.

-10-

What a Day

The footsteps were coming up the stairs. The footsteps were clickety-clicking down the hall. The footsteps were getting closer. And closer.

What is Rowena doing home?

"Quick! Hide!" said Clyde.

“Don’t worry. She won’t know it’s us with our masks on.”

But Bunny and Clyde hid anyway. They peered out from under the bed. Bunny tried not to twitch a whisker. Clyde tried to tell his tail not to thump.

Rowena hopped into the room. Her piggy bank was knocked over on its side. She took in the pile of pennies on her bed. Her eyes grew as big as quarters.

Then she spied with her beady eyes a pair of bunny ears and a striped face peering out from under the bed.

"Bunny and Clyde!" said Rowena, flapping her wings. "Get out here this second!"

Not again! Bunny and Clyde were caught red-handed. Red-*pawed*. They would never be in Rowena's good books again.

Bunny looked at Clyde. Clyde looked at Bunny. *How does she know it's us?*

The two baddies came out with their paws up.

"R-r-r-owena!" Clyde stammered. "What are you doing here?"

"I forgot my lunch," said Rowena. "I was in the kitchen when I heard a thump. What are *you* doing here? Nice masks, by the way."

Bunny did some fast-talking. "You, er, invited us."

"You always say we're welcome anytime," Clyde reminded her.

Rowena sized them up. Then she saw right through them, to her piggy bank on the bed, next to the pile of pennies. At last she spoke. "I thought the day would never come when my piggy bank was full."

Bunny's shoulders slumped. Her insides felt all cattywampus.

Clyde's whiskers drooped and his tail lost its thump.

Bunny and Clyde felt bad. Not the good kind of bad. The bad kind of bad. Rotten to the core.

Rowena's feathers were ruffled. "How did you ever do it?" she asked.

"It was just your classic breaking and entering," Clyde admitted. "Well, entering and breaking, really."

Bunny held up the spoon. "And we used this," she confessed.

Rowena let out a chirrup. "How can I ever thank you?"

Thank them?

"I've been saving up to buy penny candy. My piggy bank is full, but I couldn't for the life of me figure out how to get the pennies out without breaking the bank."

"Um, you're welcome?" said Clyde.

"How can I repay you?" Rowena chirped. "I have to think of a reward."

"Reward?" said Bunny, pricking up her ears.

"Reward?" said Clyde, swishing his bushy tail.

Rowena tapped her foot. Her eyes flashed. "I seem to remember that you two like penny candy too, right?"

"I dream of candy lipstick and peanut butter kisses," said Bunny.

"I never met a peppermint lump I didn't like," said Clyde.

"Well, aren't you the sweet talkers," said Rowena. "That settles it."

Bunny turned to Clyde. "Are you thinking what I'm thinking?"

"Are you thinking what I'm thinking?" asked Clyde.

"To the penny candy store!" they said at the same time.

As they were about to leave, Bunny and Clyde couldn't help noticing how lonely and empty Rowena's bank looked. Bunny slid her bubble gum comic into Rowena's bank. Clyde left his bottle cap behind.

Bunny and Clyde rode with Rowena in their bike basket to the penny candy store. Rowena rewarded them with all sorts of penny candy, from jawbreakers and wax lips to fireballs and root-beer barrels. They loaded their loot into the dewlap bag.

PENNY
CANDY
PENNY
CANDY
1¢
1¢
1¢
1¢
1¢

★ ★ ★

When the day was done, Bunny and Clyde made their way back to the hideout and emptied their loot all over the floor.

They hung up their masks. They hung up the dewlap bag.

Bunny put on her bunny slippers. Clyde put on his stocking cap. They stretched out in front of the pot-bellied stove, savoring one last root-beer barrel before bedtime.

"I'm full," said Bunny, rubbing her tummy.

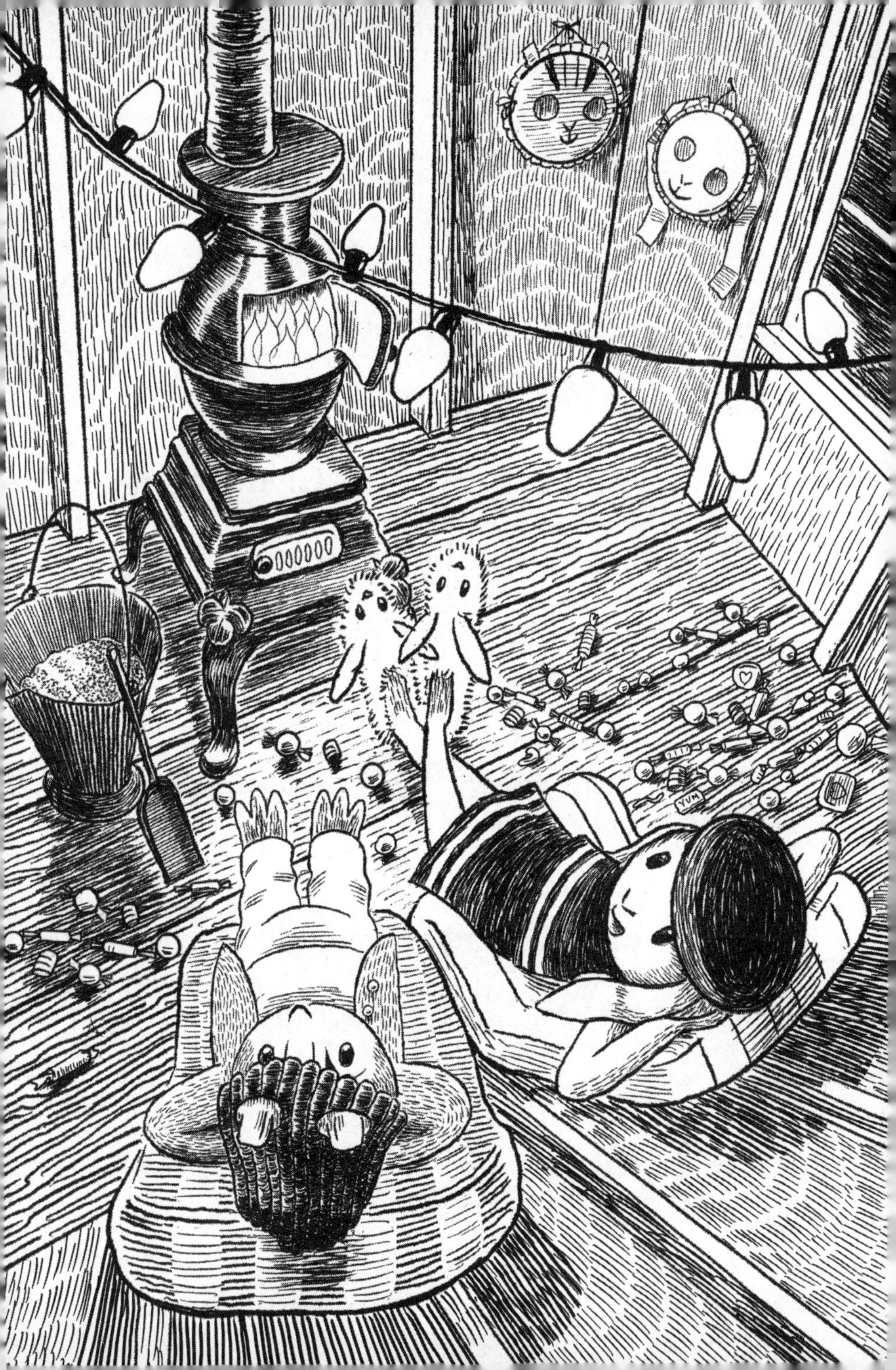
YUM

"Full of penny candy?" said Clyde.

"*And* full of Experience," said Bunny. "What. A. Day. Robbing a bank was almost a *cat*astrophe!"

"*Dog*gone right," said Clyde. "But Rowena sure was happy that we were able to get her pennies out without breaking the bank."

The fire warmed Bunny's whiskers and toasted Clyde's toes.

"We did good today, don't you think?" asked Bunny, yawning.

"Not bad. Not bad at all," said Clyde, his eyes growing heavy.

“As a famous writer once said . . .” Bunny started.

“Life is too short for bad books?” said Clyde.

"Nope," said Bunny. "All's well that ends well." She started to doze.

"Roger that," said Clyde. He began to nod off.

"What can we get up to tomorrow?" asked Bunny.